The Chaotic Crow

A Topsy-Turvy Flight through Change

By Patrick T. Finley

with editors Kelsey Schurer
and Agata Antonow

Illustrated by

Nathan Lueth

Part One:
Too Much Change

For Logan, CHANGE was like a *big, scary crow* just waiting to steal something SHINY. Something Logan *loved*.

Lately, everything around Logan was CHANGING. He had said goodbye to all his friends, classes, and teachers because his parents put him in a new school.

And Grandma Ellie had just left her farmhouse for a new home. All the MEMORIES Logan had made at Grandma's old house would be gone too.

Grandma Ellie's new home was NOTHING like Logan imagined.

Logan asked, *"What's Smart Living?"*

Smart Living is a life that's lived smart! I am one of many "smart" techs at Vitalia. There's also infrared technology, which scans you to see if you have a temperature, and other gadgets that are very helpful—just like me!

VITALIA
SMART LIVING

When Logan got sick, Grandma Ellie would bring him a hot cup of sassafras tea. She didn't have a robot or a computer or internet. And now EVERYTHING in her new home was smart?

No, Logan did not like CHANGE.

He did not like his face to FROWN.

Right then a puppy **jumped** into Grandma Ellie's arms!

My name is Gina Ballerina. **Welcome!**
I'm off to take Bella for a walk.

The puppy kissed
Grandma Ellie goodbye.

Logan did not like CHANGE; no, he did not!
He did not like his ears feeling RED HOT.

As Gina Ballerina and Bella twirled away, Logan overheard people talking about things to do here.
Someone even said they had "learning circles."

In the bistro, Grandma Ellie sat with some new friends.

Hi, I'm Dr. Vlad, the wellness director.

And I'm Constable Carolyn, chief connection officer. I help connect people who like the same things, whether that's books, art, learning circles, or Jewish studies. *Everyone's welcome here!*

Too busy making friends, Grandma didn't even notice when Logan sat down at the table.

BREAKFAST
served all day

DAILY SPECIAL
starting at 11:00 a.m.

Beef Ravioli

Portabel

splash!

Grandma Ellie jumped—
—into the pool. As she swam farther away,
Grandma Ellie became smaller and smaller...

I can't even see her anymore . . .

No, Logan did not like CHANGE.
He did not like hearing his heart
go THUMP-THUMP-THUMP.

For such a small child.

Nooo, Grandma!
Come back!

Sure. I worry about making **new friends** here.
I worry about **getting sick**. I worry about,
one day, **leaving you**...

We all fear CHANGE sometimes.
The trick is not to let
your fear *steal away* your
COURAGE or curiosity.

But How?

Logan knew the
inky black crow was
still out there, ready to
steal from him again...

Part Two:
Chaos Comes Quickly

Logan knew that change was scary, but he also knew that Grandma Ellie always told the truth. Could this topsy-turvy world be better than he thought? Logan was ready to find out.

Before Logan could sit and ponder and pout, Grandma Ellie asked Dr. Vlad to take them on another adventure inside the Memory Neighborhood.

As we get older, some things get different whether we want them to or not. Our hair turns white, our eyes lose sight, and our brains feel less bright. For some of us, even our memory takes flight.

I don't want Grandma to forget me.

Some changes we can control—like deciding to learn to ride a bike.

Some changes we can't—like losing our memories or someone we love. But you can choose how to think about it.

Could it be that simple?
Logan wasn't so sure.

One silly moment can feel out of CONTROL...

... or can make laughter EXPLODE.

Look how happy Grandma was!

Logan had never heard Grandma laugh so much at the farm.

Maybe change wasn't all that bad...

Even though **change** stole a lot of things today,
Logan didn't mind because he had *gained* stuff
he didn't even know he was missing.

The End

Inky's Shiny Treasures

Discover the true meanings, symbols, and hidden gems uniquely placed throughout this story.

Meet Our Community

*The people you met in these pages are inspired by **real** people who make up the heart and soul of Vitalia communities:*

Logan

Logan is Pat's youngest son, and he works at the Vitalia communities as a writer, editor, and research analyst. He likes to collect fountain pens, play *Dungeons & Dragons*, and work on his graphic novel. As a child, Logan was curious, constantly climbing on furniture to explore the world. Logan did not like change, not at all.

Grandma Ellie

Pat's mother, Grandma Ellie, was an ER nurse who worked nights for a small-town hospital. She's a great listener, a hard worker, and the family cheerleader. For a little while, Pat's family had a farm, and Ellie would do most of the work "raising a million chickens." As a Vitalia volunteer, she places flowers on every table in the bistro and dining room.

Inky

During Pat's childhood, his family rescued a crow with a broken wing and named him Inky. Inky loved to steal shiny jewelry from Mrs. Shank, Pat's babysitter, and hide it on top of the fridge. Once, Inky landed on Mrs. Shank's head, but she sprayed him with the watering hose, and he never bothered her again.

Gina Ballerina

Gina, Pat's wife and best friend, is as elegant and graceful as a ballerina. She was actually a gymnast and has great grace and style. She grew up in a horse country suburb and loves animals. She's rescued over two thousand dogs and loves to help anyone in need. Bella is her dog, and Tinker was Grandma Ellie's.

Queen V and King K

Queen Victoria and King Konstantin both immigrated from Ukraine to America. They are married, and as Pat says, "truly some of the funniest and brightest people" he and Gina know. Victoria is a social butterfly and before you know it, could be Queen of Vitalia too!

Mighty Mario

Mighty Mario is a blend of two Marios! One Mario is a cantankerous, entertaining, poker-playing, joke-telling resident whom everyone gets a kick out of. The other Mario is our president of Vitalia communities, an immigrant from Uruguay who is a great servant leader and loves both soccer and his grandmother.

Dr. Vlad

Dr. Vlad came to this country from Russia years ago and is a close friend of Pat and Gina. In this book, he represents the care partners who help Vitalia community members enjoy vibrant health and wellness. Dr. Vlad is also a doctor in real life and loves lamb plov.

Constable Carolyn

Carolyn lives at Vitalia and loves to take part in activities, encouraging others to join in—that's why she's a "constable," taking charge as a leader of the communities! Her big project right now is creating biographies of people who live at Vitalia, so everyone can get to know each other.

Laughing Lenny

Lenny is from Hollywood and was born to be on stage. He loves to film fun stuff that happens in the communities and makes everyone laugh. Can you spot him with his handlebar mustache and camera phone? He's one of many people who work at Vitalia to make the communities really special.

Robin

Although not a bird in real life, Robin is Pat's sister, who loves animals. She begged to keep Inky as a pet crow when they rescued him, and her love for animals was so great, Pat says, "Dad bought a horse farm." Her personality is bright and full of life. Like the bird, Robin is a symbol of community, family, and new beginnings.

Corporal Jim

Corporal Jim, Vitalia's first resident, was an American war hero who has recently passed away. A proud WWII vet who served in the South Pacific, he was a part of the original community's ribbon cutting ceremony, complete with a salute and flag raising. He proudly wore his uniform for special events.

The Real MVP Michelle

Michelle works with Pat and helped offer advice, guidance, and support in the writing of this book. Her cheerfulness and perseverance kept us all going, especially Pat.

Anna Alpaca

Anna Alpaca is actually called "Anna Banana." The wife of Dr. Vlad, Anna came over to America while Vlad was serving in the Russian military. Anna hopes to have a real alpaca farm someday. Meanwhile, she is busy lawyering and visiting alpaca farms.

Diplomat Dorothy

One of the most charismatic people Pat has ever known, eighty-nine-year-old Dorothy has been, along with her husband, a diplomat of five African countries. She's an inspiration to her family and everyone around her. She's always smiling, makes friends all over the world, and is an excellent dancer, as well as a brilliant mind.

Khari

Khari is Dorothy's grandson. His name means "prince" in Swahili, and he loves being active outdoors. No wonder he loves to visit Vitalia and play outside with the alpacas!

Isaac

Vitalia comes together as a community in caring! Isaac is a nine-year-old boy who couldn't walk and needed a big operation to use his legs again. The community has come together to make sure he can get the medical care he needs. Now, Isaac can not only walk but dance with Dorothy and play soccer with Mario too!

Wallpaper Wendy

A woman entrepreneur and, along with her husband Rick, a dear friend of Pat and Gina, Wendy has played a huge part in creating the spectacular smart homes that feel like "home." So many of us have experienced more lifeless-looking environments for senior living. Wendy's magical talent creates an environment that's inviting, mesmerizing, and unique for people of all ages.

Teacher Tom

Tom is Pat's father. Once a teacher and a principal of a small-town middle school, Tom left education to join fast-paced corporate America. After over fifty years, at age eighty-six, he has returned to his beloved education field by heading the Vitalia Scholars Advisory Board. He works full-time to this day. Can you spot him in the background of a chaotic and colorful classroom, helping Logan learn something new?

Take a Walk through Vitalia

When you first walk into a Vitalia community, you might notice it's like a nice resort!

There's a beautiful mature tree outside where people gather around, a lovely courtyard, gardens full of gnomes to make everyone smile, and superb apartments with quality details (like granite counters). There is a dining area, a demonstration kitchen, and a Napa Valley wine tasting room where you can hold parties or have a trained, professional chef prepare gourmet meals. Or you can grab a quick bite at the bistro.

In our Memory Neighborhood, you'll notice real carpet (where there's usually hard floors) and a digital screen that plays each resident's favorite images right outside their door. Here, everything is about luxurious touches and helping everyone hold on to their best memories. This place is designed for families to visit often, enhancing the well-being of their loved ones.

Here's what you might not notice at first: Vitalia is Smart Living. Vitalia has learning circles, as well as partnerships with colleges and the Rock & Roll Hall of Fame. Whether you love to read classics or jam to vintage rock, there are many fun things to experience.

That's not the only smart thing. Rooms in Vitalia have sensors, so if you live here and suddenly have a higher temperature or start to feel a little sick, we can get a doctor or someone to come and talk to you—sometimes before you even know you're sick! Vitalia is always looking for new tech to enhance its community and inspire the future.

At Vitalia, it's all about creating connections and belonging to a community. There's family-style hangout pods in the recreational area, outdoor barbeques, art classes, and iPads available for virtual fun. Grandkids *love* to visit, and some children want to move right in! (Maybe Logan?)

Did You Notice These Things?

Here is a list of hidden symbols throughout the book! Can you find them all?

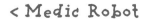

< Medic Robot

Vitalia communities love smart technology, like iPads and smart wristwatches for exercise, which helps provide the safest environment possible for all community residents. You've probably never seen a floating chair or medic robot, but Vitalia looks to the future where this ideal may surely be possible for many generations of people living together in one place.

Gnomes >

Vitalia communities all have garden gnomes because they make us smile!

Scholars >

Vitalia communities offer a scholars program to all who are eager to learn and grow! This program features learning circles, which can be anything from book clubs to Jewish culture groups, as well as partnerships with universities. Pat's eighty-six-year-old father, Tom, is a huge help in guiding the scholars program. Hint: Look for the little graduation cap on the Vitalia logo.

^ Playing Cards

You might have noticed Logan lamenting a card game called *solitaire*, which is often played alone. While this card game symbolizes isolation and loneliness, the poker game Grandma Ellie joins with Mighty Mario represents community, intellectual stimulation, and fun at Vitalia, where everyone can play together!

^
Rainbows

Rainbows symbolize the inclusive
atmosphere of all Vitalia communities,
as well as the promise to uplift and
encourage one another. Everyone is
welcome here!

< American Flags

Many Vitalia residents have seen a lot of change—
from immigrating to America and starting new
lives, to seeing the first man walk on the moon,
to standing in line for the polio vaccine, and
fighting in two or three wars! We are proud of
their patriotism and appreciate their stories.

Music >

Vitalia communities originated in Ohio and celebrate the
musical roots of Cleveland's Rock & Roll Hall of Fame. See if you
can spot the live bands, instruments, and dancing throughout
the residences. Music has a way of
bringing us all together and
rejuvenating old, fun memories.

< Nyssa

Did you notice Nyssa in
the story? She's not based
on a real person, but
her name means "new
beginnings" or "friendly elf."
Logan certainly needed a
new beginning—do you
think maybe the gnomes
sent a friendly elf to make
Logan feel less alone?

Chaos Can

This book was written in past tense on every
page—except for one! Hint: there's lots of
chaos going on. The reason behind this
shift in tenses is to show the power of true
transformation. When we experience changes
in our lives, everything feels a little topsy-
turvy—like it's happening *right now* and *forever*.
We wanted to reflect that present-to-future
feeling with not only the pictures in this book,
but the words too.

Why the Chaotic Crow?

Did you know that seeing a crow isn't bad luck at all? The crow symbolizes transformation and change in many cultures and legends. Crows are very smart and have the ability to remember and recognize faces. They can even make and use tools! In Native American folklore, crows can be a sign of good luck, wisdom, or even a little mischief. In some Celtic traditions, crows are messengers harboring the secrets of life in their feathers.

For Logan, Inky the crow brings mischief along with change. Logan sees Grandma Ellie's new home as chaotic and perhaps even a little (or a lot) unwelcome. Eventually, Logan realizes that change can be good—it's all about the wisdom to remain positive, no matter what (even when it feels like we've been pooped on, we can still laugh about it).

When a little bird, Robin, comes onto the page, her mere presence helps to balance out these chaotic feelings by reminding Logan that friendship and community and love keep us grounded, even when everything else feels out of control.

In fact, Inky the crow becomes a *friend* to Logan, reminding us that most changes *can* be good, and we should embrace new transitions as new adventures. It's a good idea to borrow some of that wisdom of the crow and ask, "What can I learn and gain from this change in my life?" Inky would say that everything can be gained—and probably placed in a nest too.

Author's Note

First, my deepest appreciation goes to my mom, known in this book as Grandma Ellie, who played such a pivotal role in my life as a boy and now as an adult. She is a quiet, humble, kind, and powerful woman of action. Her form of action was softly and inadvertently leading by example. She spent long, hard, painstaking hours on the nightshift as an emergency room nurse, dealing with condescending doctors and incorrigible and often inebriated patients at their worst. This in itself would be enough for any day. But then, she would return from this unorthodox night of work to a farm full of overactive teenagers and their army of mischievous friends always on the prowl for the next dramatic moment. She would somehow tame us by convincing us to get into moderately mischievous shenanigans that would keep us from overwhelming the very emergency room she had just escaped! She worked just as hard when she got home, as my father was also away, working an eighteen-hour day to pay the bills at our fiscally flawed farm. Thank you, Mom! I adore, respect, and appreciate you.

Second, I would like to say a few words about Logan, my youngest son (who really doesn't like change at all). There isn't a book thick enough to describe how unique and wonderful he is. His complexity, depth of knowledge, humor, work ethic, and intellect are second to none. It has taken me twenty-five years to really get to know you, Son, and I truly love what I see and experience every day when I have the pleasure of being with you.

Third, let me show my true and heartfelt appreciation for our awe-inspiring residents at Vitalia Inspirational Living Communities. A few years back, I abandoned my "deal-junkie" life as a real estate developer to create Vitalia and The V Living Experience communities because I could see that there truly was—and is—a void in properly serving our aging population. I believe that we have a chance to make a significant difference in the lives of hundreds by creating experiences that *fulfill* and *empower* as opposed to *provide* and *disempower*. Our society has fallen into the trap of rendering our aged population as seemingly obsolete and valueless. Nothing could be further from the truth. Although it is human nature to dispel an uncomfortable vision of ourselves being less meaningful and able, we have the opportunity to replace that vision with an even more empowering vision—one that is *full of life*. This book is as much for my beloved residents as it is for children. Thank **you** for imparting so much wisdom and creating a better future for us all!

Fourth, an energetic "Thank you!" goes to my editors, Kelsey Schurer and Agata Antonow, for artfully placing words and concepts where they belong and for being with me every step of the way. The meaning and experience of this book are so much better with your professional and compassionate input.

Finally, thank you to the real life "cast of characters" featured in this book. Each of you are carefully housed in this book because you have profoundly influenced me, entertained me, taught me, and properly harassed me. I dearly love each and every one of you.

About the Author

Founder and chairman of OMNI Smart Living, Vitalia Inspirational Living, and The V Living Experience, Pat Finley aims to bring the fullness of life to everyone he encounters. With a background in finance, real estate, developments and construction, and consulting, Pat has chaired the Cleveland Young Presidents' Organization, served as president of Cleveland's Commercial Real Estate Association, and chaired the board of North Coast Community Homes.

He is also an active commercial jet airplane and helicopter pilot, and in 2014, he and his seventy-nine-year-old father climbed Mount Kilimanjaro. He believes in chasing after that "vista view," no matter what age.

Pat's first book, *Spinning Into Control*, takes an in-depth look into how survivors overcome their most difficult moments and, through facing adversity and coming out the other side, experience gratitude and a fuller sense of life. *The Chaotic Crow* is his second book.

Writers of the Round Table Press
PO Box 1603, Deerfield, IL 60015
www.roundtablecompanies.com

Printed in the United States of America
First Edition: December 2021
10 9 8 7 6 5 4 3 2 1

Library of Congress Cataloging-in-Publication Data
The chaotic crow: a topsy-turvy flight through change
/ Patrick T. Finley.—1st ed. p. cm.
ISBN Hardcover: 978-1-61066-097-6
ISBN Paperback: 978-1-61066-098-3
ISBN Digital: 978-1-61066-099-0
Library of Congress Control Number: 2021949744

Writers of the Round Table Press and the logo
are trademarks of Writers of the Round Table, Inc.

Illustrator: **Nathan Lueth**
Layout/Typographer: **Christy Bui**
Editors: **Kelsey Schurer, Agata Antonow**
Proofreaders: **Adrian Bumgarner, Sheila Harris**
Project Managers: **Keli McNeill, Sunny DiMartino**

CPSIA information can be obtained
at www.ICGtesting.com
Printed in the USA
BVHW021453220122
626568BV00001B/1